DRAGON KINGDOM
of Wrenly

SHADOW HILLS

By Jordan Quinn
Illustrated by Ornella Greco at Glass House Graphics

LITTLE SIMON

New York   London   Toronto   Sydney   New Delhi

This book is a work of fiction. Any references to historical events, real people, or real places are used fictitiously. Other names, characters, places, and events are products of the author's imagination, and any resemblance to actual events or places or persons, living or dead, is entirely coincidental.

LITTLE SIMON

An imprint of Simon & Schuster Children's Publishing Division
1230 Avenue of the Americas, New York, New York 10020
First Little Simon edition February 2021
Copyright © 2021 by Simon & Schuster, Inc.
All rights reserved, including the right of reproduction in whole or in part in any form.
LITTLE SIMON is a registered trademark of Simon & Schuster, Inc., and associated colophon is a trademark of
Simon & Schuster, Inc. For information about special discounts for bulk purchases, please contact
Simon & Schuster Special Sales at 1-866-506-1949 or business@simonandschuster.com. The Simon & Schuster
Speakers Bureau can bring authors to your live event. For more information or to book an event, contact the
Simon & Schuster Speakers Bureau at 1-866-248-3049 or visit our website at www.simonspeakers.com.
Designed by Kayla Wasil
Text by Matthew J. Gilbert
GLASS HOUSE GRAPHICS Creative Services
Art and cover by ORNELLA GRECO
Colors by ORNELLA GRECO and GABRIELE CRACOLICI
Lettering by GIOVANNI SPATARO/Grafimated Cartoon
Supervision by SALVATORE DI MARCO/Grafimated Cartoon
Manufactured in China 1021 SCP
2 4 6 8 10 9 7 5 3
Library of Congress Cataloging-in-Publication Data
Names: Quinn, Jordan, author. | Glass House Graphics, illustrator.
Title: Shadow hills / by Jordan Quinn ; illustrated by Glass House Graphics.
Description: First Little Simon edition. | New York : Little Simon, 2021. | Series: Dragon kingdom of Wrenly; book 2
Summary: Ruskin the dragon and his friend Cinder are sent to Shadow Hills, the most mysterious place in all of Wrenly
under false pretenses by sinister forces.
Identifiers: LCCN 2020024870 (print) | LCCN 2020024871 (eBook) | ISBN 9781534475038 (paperback)
ISBN 9781534475045 (hardcover) | ISBN 9781534475052 (eBook)
Subjects: LCSH: Graphic novels. | CYAC: Graphic novels. | Dragons–Fiction. | Fantasy.
Classification: LCC PZ7.7.Q55 Sh 2021 (print) | LCC PZ7.7.Q55 (eBook) | DDC 741.5/973–dc23
LC record available at https://lccn.loc.gov/2020024870

Contents

Chapter 1
We Now Return to Flatfrost 6

Chapter 2
After the Sun Rose 22

Chapter 3
No Quest Would Be Complete 39

Chapter 4
Later 53

Chapter 5
Who Are These Statues Of? 67

Chapter 6
See You on the Other Side 81

Chapter 7
Meanwhile 95

Chapter 8
I Tracked You 105

Chapter 9
Word Had Spread 118

Chapter 10
One Enchantress Alone 128

Chapter 1

We now return to Flatfrost on that cold, cursed day...

TIPTOE

TIPTOE

A few doors down from the kitchen...

SHHHHHHUP

...a secret meeting is taking place.

TIPTOE TIPTOE

TIPTOE TIPTOE

TIPTOE TIPTOE

A firestorm headed for Wrenly? We haven't had one of those since I was Lucas's age.

I remember that well...the blazing winds, the constant raining fire.

13

14

GASP

I was thinking we could send... RUSKIN.

What do you think?

See?
He has no
idea.

Things just
keep getting
weirder and
weirder around
here.

21

Another chance to be a hero, and I'm here for it.

Nothing will stop me...

RRRRRRRRRRRRRRrrr

...except an empty stomach.

Maybe I have time for a quick *fly-n-fry...*

WOOOOOOOO

I know you're around here somewhere— oh!

Ouch!

Grrr...oh! There!

RUSTLE

RUSTLE

GAAAHHH—!

SWIPE

Yes! I got one!

CRACKLE
SIZZLE
SKSSSSSS

Don't come any closer, whoever you are. This is my breakfast, and I'm not sharing.

THUMP

Not even with an old friend?

What brings you back to Crestwood so soon?

Looking for more legends?

Looking for *lava rocks.*

What for?

There's a *firestorm* coming to Wrenly.

Our wizard said lava rocks have the power to stop it.

30

LATER...

Lava rocks are easy to find. There are plenty of them near the base of our volcano.

Did you hear something?

I did. I've been hearing things all morning.

Let's just ignore it and search on.

There's a lava rock.

How are these things going to stop a *storm?*

I've heard that they have special properties, but I don't know the details.

Rocks aren't really my thing.

How many do you need?

I guess as many as we can find.

33

Let's split up. We can cover more ground that way.

We'll meet on the other side.

Of course I get the path with boring old *normal* rocks.

I'm Ruskin.

I know. Everyone knows who you are.

The question is: Why are you here... again?

I'm searching for rocks with Cinder.

They don't have rocks back at the royal palace?

Lava rocks. I need them to stop the firestorm that's coming.

Chapter 3

No quest would be complete without... a trip into a creepy forest.

Cinder?

These paw-prints look a little big, but...I'm really hoping they're yours.

~BLINK~

ZOOM

...needs lava rocks...

...stop a firestorm...

Villinelle... I don't trust her.

'Tis true, *certain* lava rocks can stop a firestorm. But these won't.

You can come out now, RUSKIN!

But I was hidden! How did you—?

Oh, right...witchy powers.

45

...but only grow in **darkness.**

The plants, the animals, even the water—it's all enchanted...

...by a **spellscape** that contains the natural within the supernatural.

Shadow Hills.

The lava rocks you seek are there.

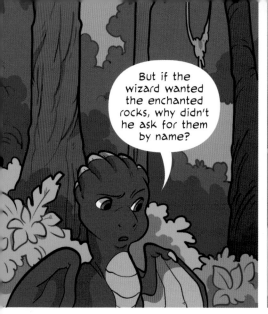

But if the wizard wanted the enchanted rocks, why didn't he ask for them by name?

Probably because he doesn't know about them.

Shadow Hills is a secret place known only to dragonkind.

A magical realm for dragons that I've never heard of before?

LET'S GO!

What are the dragons who live there like?

Are they kind? Savage? Cranky when they're hungry?

They're... not friendly to outsiders.

Just tell them your wizard found out about the Shadow Hills and sent you there for help.

So...lie to them?

They're prideful. A royal request from the palace will make them feel important.

Remember, scarlet dragon, not everyone is as important as you.

Besides...

...what's one little white lie in a realm full of dark shadows?

POOF

It's settled then...We're going to the magical shadow-realm place!

Woo-hoo!

If it means getting what we need to stop the firestorm, then...

...I'm in.

We should take Groth with us! He loves collecting rocks.

Absolutely *not.* The shadow dragons don't want too many visitors.

Another reason why you won't find the hills on any map.

How are we supposed to find it then...?

Magic?

You dare mock me, young'un?

No, not at all! We always appreciate your help, Villinelle.

51

Chapter 4

LATER...

Ruskin and Cinder flew to a secluded place hidden behind a wall of clouds...

Very few had gone there before. Even fewer had come back.

Eh, c'mon, Mr. Adventure. The entrance to Shadow Hills can't be too far.

That's weird: I don't hear birds. Or water. Or anything.

It's totally silent.

That's good. That means nothing's following us.

I'm not so sure about that.

Villinelle said we'd know the entrance when we saw it...

...and this looks like the entrance to a very mysterious place to me.

Wanna go first?

You know it. Follow me!

GULP

Shadows...

Hills...

I think we're in the right place!

What...

...is...

...happening to me?

here's nothing I
n do. That's just
hat happens to
dragons here.

Her color
will return
when she
leaves our
realm.

Her voice
will return
shortly.

She probably
feels like she's
underwater and
can't swim up.

...

Is that
how you feel?
It sounds
terrible.

You learn
to live with
it after a
while.

What
brings you
to the Shadow
Hills, my scarlet
friend?

63

We're here searching for enchanted lava rocks.

I can't help you with that.

But our enchantress, Prudense, can.

Do you want me to take you to her?

Are you still up for this?

Lead the way, Paxon.

Does the sun ever come out here?

This is sunny for us.

Oh.

Chapter 5

Just then Ruskin and Cinder discovered that things in this **gray** shadow realm...

...weren't so **black** and **white**.

Please don't let me turn into a living statue.

They're not statues! They're dragon like you and m just *different*.

Oh my...

I present to you...the scarlet dragon!

...it really is HIM!

Pleasure to meet you.

And you too!

It is an honor.

The honor is mine.

Villinelle was wrong...shadow dragons ARE friendly.

SO friendly. Each one friendlier than the last.

I feel bad we have to lie to them.

I feel terrible about it.

Greetings, I am Ruskin of Wrenly.

Why are you talking to my stone idol?

I am the one they call Prudense.

I just can't figure this place out.

I am Cinder—he's Ruskin.

We're here on an urgent mission from the palace.

What can I do for the palace?

There's a firestorm coming to Wrenly.

And we are here to ask for enchanted lava rocks to stop the storm. Can you help us?

You're certain the palace requested enchanted lava rocks? From Shadow Hills?

What's one little white lie...?

Yes. We are here for the enchanted lava rocks, to stop the storm and save Wrenly.

Chapter 6

See you on the other side!

Ow!

THUD

I thought lightning never struck the same place twice?

This is no normal place.

Let's get out of here while we still can.

WHOOOOOOSH

Once the lightning passed, everything suddenly became a lot clearer.

That's weird. We're out of the Shadow Hills, but our rocks still look gray.

Shouldn't they have changed color when you did?

I don't know.

But I know someone who does.

Why should I believe you? Is this another one of your little white lies?

Watch your tongue!

Ruskin!

What? Lying is wrong, and she made us lie to those nice dragons. And I just...don't believe her.

Ha! Nice?! Those shadow dragons would swallow up your color permanently if they could.

I don't believe you.

Then believe this: I will do anythi to protect Wrer even if I have lie to do it.

91

Let us return home while we still can.

WHOOOOOOSH

LATER...

Cinder's cousin Groth wasn't pleased to see her.

You are the worst.

You went on an adventure with Ruskin involving ROCKS...

...and you didn't even invite me

Oh no. Am I turning gray AGAIN?

GASP Where's Ruskin right now?

On his way to the palace with the rocks.

We've got to stop him!

I don't know what kind of rocks he has, but those do not sound like lava rocks. And the wrong rocks used in a wizard's spell can destroy Wrenly!

Chapter 7

Meanwhile...just above the palace...it became an awful, rainy night for a dragon's flight.

The rocks... they've finally changed...

Well done, Ruskin!

You've saved us, my boy!

Good luck...I guess?

We don't need luck anymore. We have lava rocks!

RUSKIIIIIIN!

Hey, guys!

Stop!

Stop... bathing?

No! Stop everything! Don't give the rocks away.

99

We still need the real rocks.

Wrenly's doomed. And it's all my fault.

SPLAAASH

Did you guys hear that?

RUSTLE

I definitely heard someone.

Who's there?

104

Chapter 8

I tracked you to Shadow Hills. I stole the enchanted lava rocks.

Then it is YOU who's doomed us.

Save your doom and gloom for another story.

The rocks I ve you won't ing any harm to Wrenly.

What are you talking about?

What's a Crestwood mud rock? Only a powerful magic spell could unlock the answer to one of dragonkind's most sacred questions.

Dissipatum tempestus, scidit petram, eye of newt and ala-kazaaam!

ZAP

Poop. Why is it always poop?

Ewwwww. That's disgusting!

HA-HA-HA-HA!

He's right. An incantation over dragon poop won't do anything but smell really bad. But it also won't help stop the storm.

This isn't funny. What about the firestorm that's coming? Did you think of that when you stole our rocks?

I—I—no I didn't thi about tha

108

But Cinder didn't believe him. She would do anything to get the rocks back...

Anything to save Wrenly...

Gotcha!

CLAAAANG

You got strong.

I've always been strong!

Something's wrong!

Fly fast, Groth!

Dive, dive, dive!

BAM! BAM!

As Ruskin realized where they'd all landed, it was already too late.

Rus—

Oh no.

They were in more trouble than ever, without a **shadow** of a doubt.

Chapter 9

Word had spread through the Shadow Hills that visitors had fallen from the sky.

Prudense sensed it was something more than that.

118

The enchanted lava rocks were *stolen*, you say?

Yes. We're not sure who has them now. The dragon who stole them from us is... gone.

In the wrong hands, enchanted lava rocks can do terrible damage. They are extremely powerful.

I read about that in my book!

Groth! You can speak!

Hold my book? This thing weighs a ton all of a sudden.

I feel like a whale is sitting on me. Underwater.

You get used to it.

Can you give us more enchanted lava rocks? I can rush them back to the palace...

What we gave you was all we had.

Could we make more?

It's possible, but... they won't be enough to fully absorb the storm, which has strengthened now that it has been allowed to get so close.

I would need to do the enchantment on red lava rocks.

We don't have any red rocks here, I'm afraid. They all turned gray long ago and will never glow red again.

I'm not so sure about that...

GASP

What enchantment is this?

Maybe.

But this strange *reaction* that happens, it doesn't last long.

If color returns only during your touch...

...then you'd have to be holding the rocks. *Inside* the firestorm. Which you cannot do.

That would be far too dangerous.

Chapter 10

One enchantress alone cannot make new lava rocks. It takes a village...

Heave ho! Put your backs into it!

Start with heavy sand from the bottom of a well, and stir frequently with cooled lava over low heat.

Add a dash of magic!

Behold! Enchanted lava rocks.

128

Something's happening!

135

Meanwhile, back on Crestwood...

What's in store for Ruskin and his friends next? Find out in . . .

Meanwhile, in a cave not far from there...

Every time he laughs, it's like he's laughing at me.

At *us.*

Ruskin has become a hero.

And we've let it happen.